• Monica Wellington •

Bunny's SNOWFLAKE FIRST

SCHOLASTIC INC.
New York Toronto London Auckland Sydney
Mexico City New Delhi Hong Kong Buenos Aires

Cold wind blows. Swoosh, whoosh.
Winter is coming soon.

Look—a snowflake!
Is everyone ready for winter?

Not yet. Squirrel and chipmunk gather acorns. Hurry, hurry.

Not yet. Snowflakes swirl.
Bear licks honey, sticky sweet.

Not yet. Raccoon digs for pinecones.

Rustle, rustle. Scratch, scratch.

Almost. Mouse and skunk find

fruit and berries. Nibble, nibble.

Hush, hush. Storm is ending.
Everyone is ready for winter now.

Warm and cozy, it's time to sleep.
Are you coming, bunny?